A BOY WITH BREAD AND FISHES

A BOY WITH BREAD AND FISHES

XULON PRESS

Xulon Press
2301 Lucien Way #415
Maitland, FL 32751
407.339.4217
www.xulonpress.com

© 2018 by Albert Rowlands

All rights reserved solely by the author. The author guarantees all contents are original and do not infringe upon the legal rights of any other person or work. No part of this book may be reproduced in any form without the permission of the author. The views expressed in this book are not necessarily those of the publisher.

Printed in the United States of America.

ISBN-13: 978-1-54563-562-9

There is a boy here who has five barley loaves and two fish; but what good are these for so many. (John 6:9)

A boy with bread and fishes

Hi, my name is Aaron and I am ten years old. I have two brothers, John who is eight, and Mark who is six. Mom takes care of us by herself, since Dad was killed by the Roman soldiers for not getting his donkey out of their way fast enough. Since Dad's passing, Mom had to take any work she could get to keep the family together. I really feel sorry for her; Mom comes home from work so tired, her work includes getting water from the town well, cleaning houses, and tending to the shrubs and garden, when she arrives home immediately starts supper for us. She is such a wonderful mother.

One memorable morning, before Mom left for work, she turned and looked at me and said, "Aaron, I want you to go to the market today and get some bread and fish for supper. But, you must be home before dark." Mom knew how I liked to play with all of the other kids my age, which cause me to stay at the marketplace too long. Mom said, "I have to work all day. I will not have time to go to the market, before it closes, to get the bread and fish."

Mom gave me a few pennies and said, "Be careful; don't lose any of the pennies because that is all the money I have. Aaron, you know how hard it is for a woman who has no husband to find work. I clean houses, carry jugs of water, cultivate the flowers and vegetable gardens, and do anything else that needs to be done: and sometimes I only make a few widow mites for a full day's work (In our time a mite would equal two dollars for a twelve to sixteen-hour work day.)

"Aaron, look at all of the bread and fish, and get the freshest that you can find of each."

As she left for work just before the sun came up over the mountains toward eastern sky, then she turned and said I have to work in the garden all day.

I knew it would be well after dark before she would be home to fix supper.

Around noon, I decided it was about time for the trip to the marketplace. As I made my way toward the market, the heat of the day was already making it very hot, and the road was very dusty from the chariots and animals that traveled the same road into town.

The dust from the road would squeeze between my toes and make little puff balls of dust with each step. The sun beat down on my head, causing beads of sweat to run down my face and make little, crooked paths on my face from the dust that settled there.

With each step, the mile to town seemed longer. As the sun beat down on me, I would stop at each shade tree to cool down. I knew if I got to the market a little after noon, the bread that was baked that morning and the fish that was caught the night before would still be fresh.

When I finally arrived at the marketplace, the dust from the road had covered me from head to toe. It had even settled in my pockets, where I had the few pennies Mom gave me for the fish and bread.

I entered the marketplace, where the vendors were lined on both sides of the street. Each of the vendors were yelling at the top of their voices, "Shop here; we have the freshest bread, fish and vegetables available." As I wandered down the street, checking out each of the vendors, I stopped at several of them and almost bought their fish and bread. Then I remembered what Mom said: "Check out each of the vendors for the freshest fish and bread." So, I continued checking each vendor until I reached the last one.

The female vendor was sitting quietly behind a table and offered the freshest, allowing each shopper to judge her fish, bread and vegetables for themselves. The woman was dressed much like me, her clothes worn and threadbare; the only difference was she wasn't covered with dust like me. I asked, "When was the bread baked?"

She looked up and said to me, "You look awfully young to buy anything." I replied, "My mom sent me to buy some bread and fishes." She then asked, "Do you have any money?", to which I showed her the few pennies that Mom gave me. The woman said, "That will not buy very much; is that all you have?" I said, "Yes, that is all we have. Mom works all day to provide us with food and clothes." "Where is your father?" she asked. I answered, "My father was killed by the Roman soldiers. He did not get his donkey out of their way fast enough, and they killed him."

The woman looked at me for a few seconds, then picked up some bread and wrapped them in the cloth Mom had given me, to keep the bread from getting dusty, and placed it in my basket.

About that time, a man walked up with a large basket of fish. She turned to me quickly and said, "This is mark my husband; he just came back from fishing and these are the freshest fish in the marketplace." She then grabbed some fish from his basket, wrapped them up and put them in my basket as well.

I handed her the money that Mom gave me, knowing it was not enough money for all the bread and fish she had packed in my basket. I stood there, waiting for her to take back some of the food after seeing the money I offered. She looked at me, with fire in her eyes, and said, "I do not like the Romans as she dropped the money in my basket. Take the fish and bread, and go home."

I thought, *Wow, this much bread and fish will last us for several days!* By then, Mom will make some more money at her job.

As I walked the dusty road on the way home, looking ahead, I could see a large group of people standing on a grassy knoll. As I drew closer, I could see the crowd was a lot larger; there must have been thousands standing on the grassy knoll. There was a man standing on top of the knoll, talking to the crowd. My curiosity got the best of me, and I walked over to where the crowd was standing.

I could not hear clearly what the man was talking about, with all of the people standing in around me chattering what he had done in other places, so I drifted up the knoll until I could clearly hear what the man was saying. The people there kept looking at me, in my tattered, dust-covered clothes and carrying the basket with bread and fish in it

The man at the top of the knoll was talking about the kingdom of Heaven. He said:

> In the kingdom, there will be no more tears, no more death or pain, they will not hunger or thirst. Blessed are they who mourn, for they shall be comforted. Blessed are the merciful, for they will be shown mercy. (Matthew 5:7)

As I listened to the words that he spoke, it seemed that every word was directed straight to me. He was so interesting that I could not leave. I thought about that place called Heaven that the man speaking made sound so real and beautiful. With the killing and destruction that the Romans had brought on my family, I wanted to take Mom and my two brothers and go there. I wonder how far away it is and how long it would take us to get there.

Suddenly, a man came over to me and asked what I had in the basket. I said, "Some bread and fishes." He turned and walked to the man who was speaking to the crowd, and they both turned and looked at me. The man who had asked what I had in the basket started walking straight toward me.

Panic hit me; what if he came to take the only food for my mom and brothers? I wanted to run away from there while I still had the food in the basket. I knew that the food I had would last us a few days.

I could not run; it was as though my feet were glued to the ground. The man walked straight to me and said, "The Master wants your bread and fishes." Thoughts raced through my mind. If I gave the man my bread and fish, Mom and my two brothers would go hungry maybe for several days. What would I tell Mom about the bread and fishes? Would Mom understand, or would she be upset about my giving all the food we had to a complete stranger? Then again, how could I turn down the man they called Master, who was speaking directly to me all afternoon?

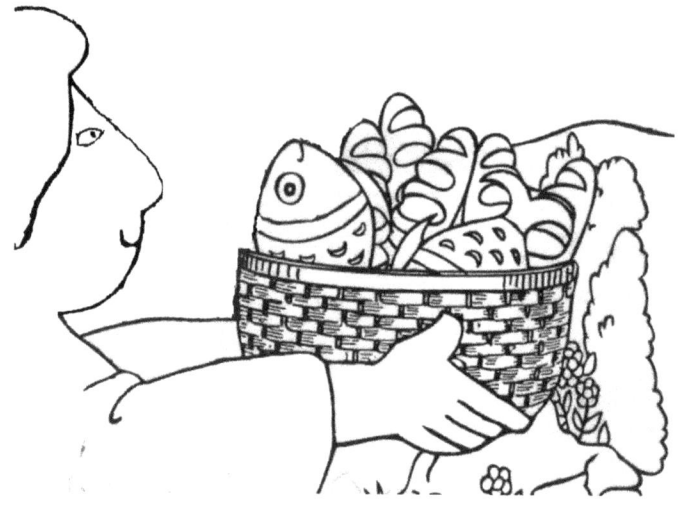

I handed the basket to the man, and he walked straight to the man the others called Master. The man they called Master took the basket, raised His face to the sky and said a prayer, "Father in heaven, bless the bread and fish to feed your children gathered here today."

He handed the basket back to the man who originally had it. The one they called Master had the people sit down in groups that looked like about fifty people to me, there must be a hundred groups, then told the man with the basket to feed the people. I chuckled to myself, as I thought *how far does he think a little bread and fishes will go*. The man fed the first group, then started feeding the second group. I thought, *where is all of that food*

coming from? I knew what was in the basket, and it would not have even feed the first group.

My mind wandered back to the man they called Master, who prayed and blessed the food. I thought this man is truly from God to feed all these people with a little bread and a few fishes. I recognized this miracle must be from God. Mom made sure we knew as much about our God as possible, we attended the services in the temple, where my brothers and I learned about GODs laws and miracles, mom went to the temple with us when she was not too tired from all of the week-long work. mom always said "what you learn in the temple will go with us the rest of our lives." I started down the knoll making my way through the crowd, on my way home, I heard a man yell, "Thank you, Jesus, for the food!" I thought that must be the name of the man they called Master.

My thoughts then turned to my problem: Mom and my two brothers. What was I going to tell them about the food that I bought at the market, with the few pennies Mom had given me? I knew Mom would never believe that a little bread and a few fishes would feed thousands of people.

As I walked slowly down the knoll, my head bent down looking at the ground. I kicked a few stones down the knoll with my bare feet. The man who took my basket caught up to me, put his hand on my shoulder and said, "The Master wants you to take the leftover food home with you." He led me up the knoll to where the Master was standing. I felt as if thousands of people were looking at us.

The Master stooped down, looked me in the eyes and thanked me for the food. He put His hand on my head and said a prayer, "Father in heaven, bless and comfort this lad throughout his life." He stood up and said, "Aaron, take the leftover food home to your family." I looked around for my small basket, wondering how did this man they called Master know my name. I saw my little basket mixed in a bunch of other baskets. I tried to pull my basket out from all of the others.

The man called Master smiled at me and said, "All of these are yours to take home to feed your family." Some of my friends saw me there and came over to help me carry the twelve baskets home.

Just after dark, Mom came home from work and looked at the amount of food that had been brought home. Mom realized that the few pennies she had given me would never buy that much food. With panic in her eyes, her voice raised and quivering, she asked, "Did you steal all of this food from the market?" I tried to explain to Mom how a man called Master had prayed over and blessed the bread and the few fishes, and fed thousands. After all, had eaten, there was still twelve baskets left over.

The man called Master thanked me and said, "I was to take the twelve leftover baskets home," I replied. Mom looked at me as if I had stepped off of the deep end of the fishing dock. Lucky for me, some of my friends that helped me carry the twelve baskets home were still there. They all told the same story; how the Master put His hand on me and said a prayer, and thanked me for the food.Mom picked up the little basket that she had sent with me, removed the fish and bread from the basket for supper, in the bottom of the basket was the money that the store keeper had refused to keep and mixed in with our few well-worn mites was just as many new shiny coins, a smiled crossed her face as if she suspected something, then ask what is his name? mom I heard someone called Him Jesus. Mom broke into a smile that I had not seen since before our father was killed by the Romans. Mom said "I have heard many people talking about this man and how He had worked many miracles and healed the sick where ever He went, I always thought it was just talk. Now a miracle has come to our home, I now realize God has sent Jesus into this world to save us from evil one, truly this man called Jesus is the son of God." Mathew 6:13. Matthew 13:

We ate from the twelve baskets of food each day, as the weeks went by the bread and fishes were still just as fresh as the day I brought them home. I wondered how this could be. I thought about the grassy knoll, and the man called Jesus. He prayed over the bread and fishes and fed thousands,

maybe what Jesus has blessed will never go bad. Mom said "it is a miracle from our God, just thank Him for the way he fed thousands; and extended His blessing to our humble home, Aaron remember this miracle the rest of your life. Jesus will supply your needs as He has supplied food for our table."
Philippians 4:19

> By *Albert Rowlands*
> August 2016

www.ingramcontent.com/pod-product-compliance
Ingram Content Group UK Ltd.
Pitfield, Milton Keynes, MK11 3LW, UK
UKHW021903240426
12048UKWH00038B/1255